ALL NIGHT, ALL DAY:

*A Child's First Book
of African-American Spirituals*

ALL NIGHT, ALL DAY:

A Child's First Book
of African-American Spirituals

selected and illustrated by

ASHLEY BRYAN

musical arrangements by

DAVID MANNING THOMAS

Atheneum   1991   New York

Collier Macmillan Canada
Toronto

Maxwell Macmillan International Publishing Group
New York   Oxford   Singapore   Sydney

To the memory of
Arthur Duplex Wright III,
World War II comrade, scholar, and
dear friend:
"Angels Watching Over Thee"
—A. B.

To my wife, Gale; to our new child, Leandria;
and to the principal of Caledonia Elementary School,
Mrs. Stella Loeb-Munson
—D. M. T.

Atheneum
Macmillan Publishing Company
866 Third Avenue
New York, NY 10022

Collier Macmillan Canada, Inc.
1200 Eglinton Avenue East
Suite 200
Don Mills, Ontario M3C 3N1

First edition
Printed in Hong Kong
10 9 8 7 6 5 4 3 2 1

Library of Congress Cataloging-in-Publication Data

All night, all day: a child's first book of African-American
spirituals / selected and illustrated by Ashley Bryan.
1 score.
For voice and piano.
Includes chord symbols.
Summary: A selection of twenty spirituals, that distinctive music
from the time of slavery. Includes piano accompaniment and guitar
chords.
ISBN 0-689-31662-3
1. Spirituals (Songs)—Juvenile. [1. Spirituals (Songs)]
I. Bryan, Ashley.
M1670.A4 1991
90-753145

CONTENTS

All Night, All Day   8

Chatter with the Angels   9

Who's That a-Comin' Over Yonder   12

Somebody's Knocking at Your Door   13

This Little Light of Mine   16

Behold That Star   17

I'm a-Going to Eat at the Welcome Table   20

O When the Saints Go Marching In   21

I Stood on the River of Jordan   24

Get on Board   25

Peter, Go Ring the Bells   28

He's Got the Whole World in His Hands   29

Wade in the Water   32

There's No Hiding Place   33

The Rocks and the Mountains   36

I'm Gonna Sing   37

Open the Window, Noah   40

O Won't You Sit Down   41

Now Let Me Fly   44

Great Big Stars   45

A Note on the Spirituals   48

All Night, All Day

Arr. David M. Thomas

Chatter with the Angels

Arr. David M. Thomas

Chat-ter with the an - gels, soon in the mor - nin', Chat-ter with the an - gels, in that land!

Chat-ter with the an - gels, soon in the mor - nin', Chat-ter with the an - gels, join that band!

I hope to join that band and Chat-ter with the an - gels all day long!

I hope to join that band and Chat-ter with the an - gels all day long!

Who's That a-Comin' Over Yonder

Arr. David M. Thomas

Somebody's Knocking at Your Door

Arr. David M. Thomas

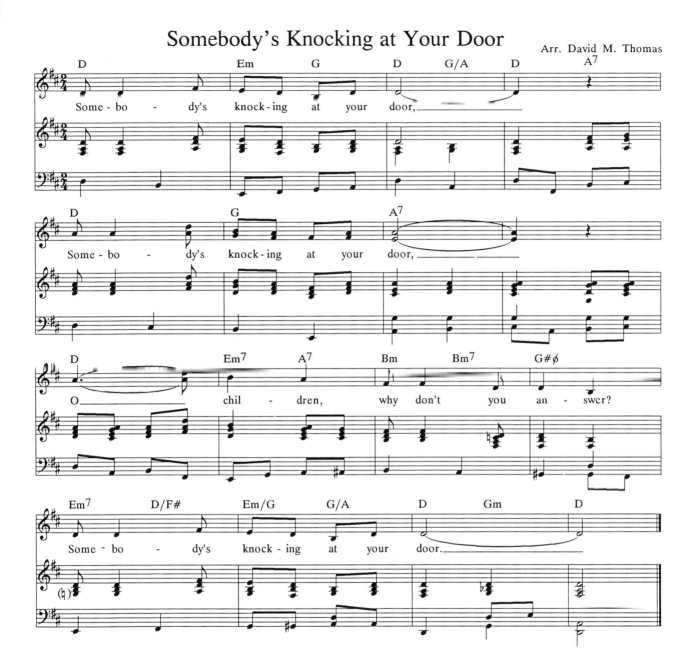

This Little Light of Mine

Behold That Star

Arr. David M. Thomas

I'm a-Going to Eat at the Welcome Table

Heavy gospel feel, medium tempo

Arr. David M. Thomas

O When the Saints Go Marching In

Arr. David M. Thomas

I Stood on the River of Jordan

With much emotion (♩ = 92)

Arr. David M. Thomas

1. I stood on the ri-ver of Jor-dan, To see the ships come sail-ing o-ver,
2. O sis-ter, you bet-ter be read-y,
3. O bro-ther, you bet-ter be read-y,

Stood on the ri-ver of Jor-dan, To see the ships sail by.
Sis-ter, you bet-ter be read-y,
Bro-ther, you bet-ter be read-y,

Refrain

O mourn-er, don't you weep! When you see the ships come sail-ing o-ver,

O mourn-er, don't you weep! When you see the ships sail by.

Get on Board

Arr. David M. Thomas

Peter, Go Ring the Bells

Arr. David M. Thomas

He's Got the Whole World in His Hands

Arr. David M. Thomas

Wade in the Water

Arr. David M. Thomas

There's No Hiding Place

The Rocks and the Mountains

Arr. David M. Thomas

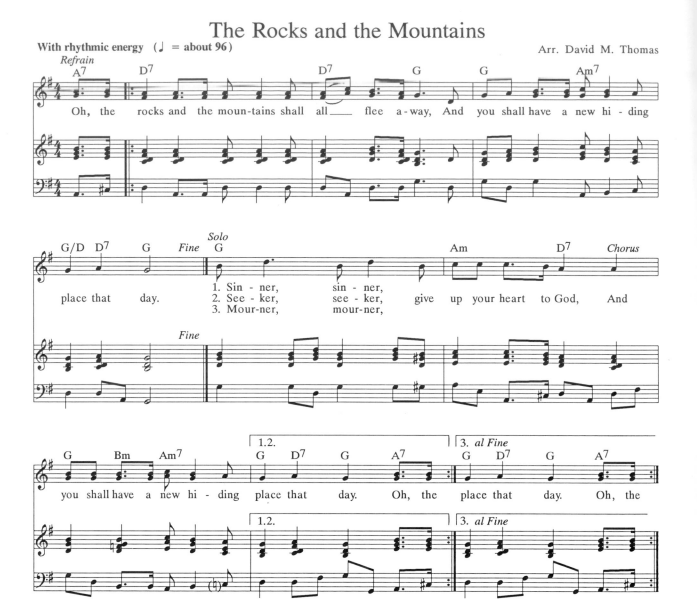

I'm Gonna Sing

Arr. David M. Thomas

Open the Window, Noah

Arr. David M. Thomas

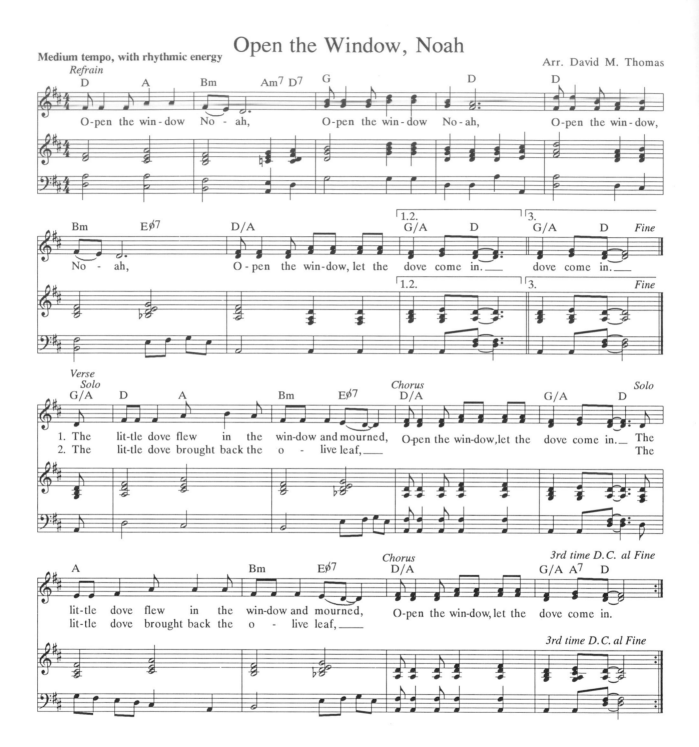

O Won't You Sit Down

Now Let Me Fly

With energy (♩ = 120)

Refrain

Arr. David M. Thomas

Now let me fly, _____ Now let me fly, _____ Now let me fly, _____ way up high, _____ Way in the mid-dle of the air. *Fine*

Verse (unis.)

Way down yon-der in the mid-dle of the field, See me wor-king at the cha-riot wheel.

Not so par-tic'-lar 'bout wor-king at the wheel, But I just want to see how the cha-riot feels.

D.C. al Fine

Great Big Stars

Arr. David M. Thomas